I Wish I Were a Pilot

Written by **Stella Blackstone**

Illustrated by **Max Grover**

Barefoot Books

I wish I were a pilot, flying in the sky.

I wish I were a balloonist,
floating high, high, high.

I wish I were
a racing driver —
race me if you dare!

I wish I were a sailor,
and could travel everywhere.

I wish I were the driver
of a big steam train.

I wish I were a cyclist,
whizzing down the lane.

I wish I were a rower,
    in a boat with gleaming oars.

I wish I were a coachman,
with a splendid coach and four.

I wish I were an astronaut, hurtling into space.

I wish I were a cowboy,
with the fresh wind in my face.

I wish I were the captain
of a yellow submarine.

I wish I could go farther
than anyone has been.

On the Move

How would you like to travel if you could choose from the many ways shown in this book? Have another look at the illustrations, read these fun facts about the different types of transport, and then decide — perhaps you'll invent something new of your own!

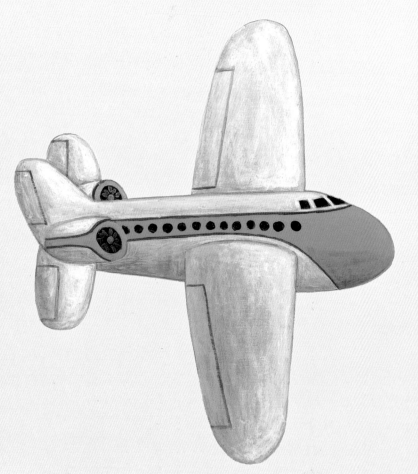

Aeroplane

People have wanted to fly for centuries, but it was not until 1903 that the Wright brothers succeeded in flying the first aeroplane in North Carolina, USA. Nowadays, a hundred years later, air travel has become universal.

Aeroplanes are kept in the sky by the flow of air over their wings, in much the same way as a kite is kept in the air by the breeze. In the early days of flying, aeroplanes were powered by propellers. Nowadays, most aeroplanes have jet engines.

Balloon

Joseph and Etienne Montgolfier designed the hot air balloon in 1783. Its passengers were a sheep, a duck and a cockerel. The first propane-powered balloon was launched in Nebraska, USA, in 1960.

Hot air balloons lift off the ground because hot air is lighter than cold air — so filling the balloon with hot air makes it lighter than the surrounding air. Balloons cannot be steered, so they travel where the wind takes them.

Racing Car

Karl Benz invented the first car in 1885. The first motor race took place in France in 1895. It was a road race from Paris to Bordeaux and was won by Emile Levassor. Formula One Grand Prix racing began in 1950 at Silverstone, in England.

Formula One racing cars are powered by very advanced petrol engines and reach speeds of over 200 mph. The fastest car in the world is the Thrust SSC. This car is powered by two aircraft jet engines and broke the world land speed record in 1997, driving across the desert at 763 mph! It travels so fast that it needs a parachute to help it stop.

Tugboat

Tugboats are small, strongly-built watercrafts which are used to tow large ships in and out of port. Early tugboats used steam power, but they are now run by diesel engines.

The first tugboat was designed and patented in 1736 by Jonathan Hulls of Gloucestershire, England, but Hulls never succeeded in building it. Alexander Hart of Scotland was the first person to actually build one, in 1801. Called the 'Charlotte Dundas', it was powered by a steam engine and a large paddle wheel. On its first and only journey, the 'Charlotte Dundas' towed two 70-ton barges almost twenty miles.

Train

Early trains were powered by steam, and the most famous of these is 'The Rocket', designed in 1829 by George Stephenson, an English engineer. Steam engines are powered by burning coal, oil or wood, which heats water in a boiler. This generates steam, which expands into cylinders and makes the wheels go round.

The railways grew very fast from the early 1800s, and helped transport people and freight in many countries. Steam engines have now been mostly replaced by diesel and electrically-powered engines, which are more efficient and can travel much more quickly.

Bicycle

Bicycles were developed throughout the 1800s, and have become one of the most popular means of transport in the world. Originally, bicycles had heavy metal frames and were uncomfortable to ride, but nowadays bicycles are made of very light metal or carbon fibre.

The pedals on a bicycle are connected to the back wheel with a chain, so that when the cyclist pedals, the bicycle moves forward. Most bicycles have gears, which the cyclist can change to make it easier to go uphill, or to go faster downhill.

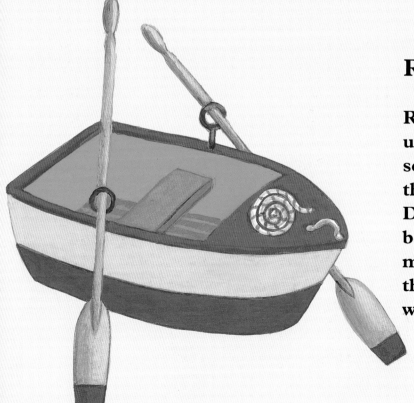

Rowing Boat

Rowing originated in Ancient Egypt and was used for transport and warfare by many early societies. Rowing as a sport became popular in the 1700s and the oldest rowing contest is the Doggetts Coat and Badge race, which has been held on the River Thames since 1715. The most outstanding rower in the world today is the English oarsman Steve Redgrave, who has won five Olympic gold medals.

Coach and Four

Coaches come in various shapes and sizes, and have been used as a means of transport for many centuries. The bigger the coach, the greater the number of horses needed to pull it. It is more usual, however, for a coach to be pulled by a pair of horses, under the guidance of a coachman.

The first stagecoach used for transporting members of the public travelled from London to Plymouth in 1658. It took nearly a week to travel two hundred and fifty miles. Stagecoaches stopped at special coaching inns on their routes so that the horses pulling them could eat, drink and rest, and be changed for fresh horses if the journey was a long one.

Space Shuttle

The first man in space was Yuri Gagarin, a Russian cosmonaut. He orbited the earth in 1961. In 1969, US astronaut Neil Armstrong became the first man to set foot on the moon.

The space shuttle uses solid fuel booster rockets to help launch it into space. These are then jettisoned high above the sea. The shuttle returns to earth as a glider and usually lands at Edwards Air Force Base in California.

Cowboy

The first cowboys came from Mexico. Known as 'vaqueros', they were men who rode horses to look after their herds of cattle. American cowboys were known for their special clothes: wide-brimmed hats to shade their eyes, and heeled boots to keep their feet in their stirrups. Cowboys often had to drive their cattle over very long distances, so they needed their horses to transport them.

William Cody, or Buffalo Bill, was a very famous cowboy. He had a travelling show called 'The Congress of Rough Riders' which made the Wild West famous.

Submarine

The first submarine was launched by Cornelius Van Drebbel in 1620, and moved at a depth of fifteen feet below the surface of the River Thames. A long time later, submarines became more sophisticated and they played a strategic part on both sides in the two World Wars. Nowadays, many submarines are nuclear powered. The first nuclear-powered submarine was called the Nautilus and it was built in 1951.

Submarines are designed to be as quiet as possible, and they are usually detected by sonar, the underwater equivalent of radar. Nuclear submarines can stay underwater for several months at a time, and have even crossed the Arctic Sea under the Polar Ice Cap.

For Erin, who will be a superstar — S. B.

For my great pals, Frank and Cynthia — M. G.

Barefoot Books
124 Walcot Street
Bath BA1 5BG

First published in Great Britain in 2005 by Barefoot Books, Ltd
This paperback edition printed in 2007

This book was typeset in 25 on 34 point Plantin Schoolbook
The illustrations were prepared in acrylics on Bainbridge board

Graphic design by Judy Linard, London
Colour separation by Bright Arts, Singapore
Printed and bound in China by Printplus Ltd

This book has been printed on 100% acid-free paper

Paperback ISBN 978-1-84686-134-5

British Cataloguing-in-Publication Data:
a catalogue record for this book is available from the British Library

3 5 7 9 8 6 4 2